The Boy Who Cried Wolf

For Jim–B. G. H.

To the boy who cried wolf–B. K.

SIMON & SCHUSTER BOOKS FOR YOUNG READERS
An imprint of Simon & Schuster Children's Publishing Division
1230 Avenue of the Americas, New York, New York 10020
Text copyright © 2006 by Simon & Schuster, Inc.
Illustrations copyright © 2006 by Boris Kulikov

SIMON & SCHUSTER BOOKS FOR YOUNG READERS is a trademark of Simon & Schuster, Inc.
Book design by Dan Potash
The text for this book is set in Uncle Stinky.
The illustrations for this book are rendered in watercolor and gouache.
Manufactured in China
2 4 6 8 10 9 7 5 3 1
Library of Congress Cataloging-in-Publication Data
Hennessy, B. G. (Barbara G.)
The boy who cried wolf / retold by B.G. Hennessy ; illustrated by Boris Kulikov.– 1st ed. • p. cm.
Summary: A boy tending sheep on a lonely mountainside thinks it a fine joke to cry "wolf" and watch the people come
running–and then one day a wolf is really there, but no one answers his call.
ISBN-13: 978-0-689-87433-8
ISBN-10: 0-689-87433-2 (hardcover)
[1. Fables. 2. Folklore.] I. Kulikov, Boris, 1966- ill. II. Title.
PZ8.2.H4215Bo 2006
398.2–dc22 2004021672

first edition

The Boy Who Cried Wolf

Retold by B. G. Hennessy
Illustrated by Boris Kulikov

Simon & Schuster Books for Young Readers
New York   London   Toronto   Sydney

There was once a shepherd.

"I am SO bored," he thought.

"All day long all I do is watch sheep. All the sheep do is eat. Not only that, all they say is baaaaaaaaaaaa."

Munch, munch, munch.

Baaaaaaaaaaaaa, answered the sheep.

"Nothing ever happens here.
"None of my friends come to play.
"I am the most bored boy in
the world," thought the shepherd.
Munch, munch, munch.
Baaaaaaaaaaaaa, answered the sheep.

"I wonder if sheep ever get bored," he thought.
He decided to teach the sheep some tricks.

He expected the sheep would be happy to learn
something new, but none of them seemed interested.
Munch, munch, munch.
Baaaaaaaaaaaaa, the sheep protested.

"What I need is a little excitement," said the shepherd.
"Well, what would be exciting? I know!" he said.
The shepherd boy jumped up from under his tree in the pasture and ran all the way into town, yelling, "WOLF! WOLF! WOLF! There is a wolf after my sheep!"

All of the townsfolk came running as fast as they could to help the shepherd boy protect his sheep.

They looked everywhere for the wolf.

No wolf in the pasture.

No wolf on the hill.

No wolf in the forest.

One of the shepherd boy's friends stayed with him for
the rest of the day to make sure the wolf was really gone.

"That was a fun afternoon," thought the shepherd boy.

But the next day . . .
Munch, munch, munch.
Baaaaaaaaaaaaa.
Life in the pasture was back to boring again.

So the shepherd boy jumped up from under his tree in the pasture and ran into town, this time yelling, "WOLVES! WOLVES! WOLVES! There are TWO wolves after my sheep!"

And, just like the day before, everyone came running lickety-split to help the shepherd boy protect his sheep.

And, just like the day before, they looked everywhere for the wolves.

No wolves in the pasture.
No wolves on the hill.
No wolves in the forest.

"They must have run away," the shepherd explained. One of the boy's friends stayed with him for the rest of the day, this time to see if there really was a wolf.

"That was another fine afternoon," thought the shepherd boy after his friend had left.

The next day, just when the shepherd boy was beginning to get bored again, he heard . . .
Lunch, lunch, lunch!

GRRRRRRRRRRRRRRRRRR

And . . .
Lunch, lunch, lunch!

GRRRRRRRRRRRRRRRRRR

And . . .
Lunch, lunch, lunch!

GRRRRRRRRRRRRRRRRRRR

And there, by the edge of the pasture,
were THREE BIG HUNGRY WOLVES!
The sheep started running in all directions.
And for the third time the shepherd
jumped up from under his tree in the
pasture and ran into town, this time
yelling, "WOLVES! WOLVES! WOLVES!
There are THREE wolves after my sheep!"

But this time, no one came to help.
This time, no one believed him.
And the shepherd boy spent the rest of the day
looking for his sheep, all by himself.